NANCY DREW
AND THE CLUE CREW®

#18

Earth Day Escapade

BY CAROLYN KEENE

ILLUSTRATED BY MACKY PAMINTUAN

Aladdin Paperbacks
New York London Toronto Sydney

🎀 ALADDIN PAPERBACKS

An imprint of Simon & Schuster Children's Publishing Division

1230 Avenue of the Americas, New York, NY 10020

Text copyright © 2009 by Simon & Schuster, Inc.

Illustrations copyright © 2009 by Macky Pamintuan

All rights reserved, including the right of reproduction in whole or in part in any form.

NANCY DREW, NANCY DREW AND THE CLUE CREW, ALADDIN PAPERBACKS, and related logo are registered trademarks of Simon & Schuster, Inc.

Designed by Lisa Vega

The text of this book was set in ITC Stone Informal.

Manufactured in the United States of America

First Aladdin Paperbacks edition January 2009

10 9 8 7 6 5 4 3 2

Library of Congress Control Number 2008928032

ISBN-13: 978-1-4169-7218-1

ISBN-10: 1-4169-7218-8

CONTENTS

ChAPTER ONE

Queen or Mean?

"Detectives like me do lots of things to help the earth," eight-year-old Nancy Drew read out loud. "My detective club, the Clue Crew, recycles our clue bags. Except the ones with icky stuff inside, like chewed-up gum or scabby Band-Aids!"

"Eww—gross!" Deirdre Shannon cried from her desk.

Nancy ignored Deirdre as she kept reading her essay, "What I Do to Help Save the Earth."

Every kid in Mrs. Ramirez's third-grade class had written an essay for Earth Week.

Earth Week was coming up, and River Heights Elementary School was planning a parade down River Street. Because Mrs. Ramirez's class had collected the most cans and bottles to recycle, they would have their own parade float.

Best of all, the student who wrote the best essay would be picked by Mrs. Ramirez to be the King or Queen of Green!

"And that's how Bess, George, and I help save the earth," Nancy finished reading. She brushed aside her reddish blond bangs, looked up, and smiled.

"Thank you, Nancy," Mrs. Ramirez said.

Bess Marvin and George Fayne both gave Nancy a thumbs-up as she walked back to her desk.

"Awesome, Nancy!" whispered George.

"Even the icky part!" Bess giggled.

"Thanks," Nancy whispered back. She was the last in the class to read her essay. As she sat down, she felt Felicity Faulkner tap her shoulder. Felicity sat in the desk behind Nancy. She was also the new kid in the class.

"I liked the part about the energy-saving light-bulbs in the Clue Crew's flashlights," Felicity whispered, leaning over. "We use only CFL bulbs at home!"

Nancy already knew. Felicity's whole essay had been about how earth-friendly her family was. Not only did the Faulkners save electricity, they saved water by flushing the toilet only when absolutely necessary.

Deirdre was grossed out by that, too!

"You all wrote excellent essays, boys and girls," Mrs. Ramirez said as she walked to the front of the classroom. "Now let's talk about the Earth Week parade."

Nadine Nardo's hand shot up. "Are you going to pick the king or queen now, Mrs. Ramirez?" she asked.

Nancy wiggled excitedly in her seat. She wanted to be the Queen of Green more than anything!

"Let's talk about the float first," Mrs. Ramirez said. "Peter, show the class what you made last night."

Peter Patino stood up. He carried something

made of colored clay to the front of the classroom.

"What's that?" asked Tommy Maron.

"I asked Peter to make a clay model of our parade float," Mrs. Ramirez explained.

The kids stretched their necks to see Peter's clay model. Nancy thought it looked a bit like a spaceship.

"Will our float be made out of clay too?" Shelby Metcalf asked.

Mrs. Ramirez shook her head. "The float will be a flatbed truck pulled by a tractor," she told the class. "And it will be decorated with the cans and bottles you collected."

Nancy raised her hand and asked, "What's that round thing in the middle?"

"It's a birthday cake," Mrs. Ramirez said with a smile. "I thought we'd celebrate the earth's birthday and call the float 'Happy Earth Day to You!'"

"Mrs. Ramirez?" Kevin Garcia asked next. "What will the cake be made of? Chocolate? Coconut? Vanilla?"

"The cake will be made out of recycled cans and cardboard," the teacher answered.

"Cans and cardboard?" said Kevin. "What good is a cake you can't eat?"

"Who cares about cake?" Deirdre said. She stood and flipped her hair over her shoulder. "Mrs. Ramirez, where will my throne—I mean—where will the king or queen's throne be on the float?"

Nancy looked sideways at Bess and George. Deirdre Shannon was used to getting everything she wanted. And now she wanted to be the Queen of Green!

"The throne will be in the back of the float," Mrs. Ramirez said. "Any other questions?"

Deirdre sat down and Quincy Taylor stood up. "I don't see my compost bin on that float, Mrs. Ramirez," he said.

"Your compost bin won't be on the float, Quincy," Mrs. Ramirez told him gently.

"But compost is important, Mrs. Ramirez!" Quincy cried. "When the old leaves, fruit, and veggie scraps rot, they feed the earth!"

"You forgot to mention the worms," George put in.

"Georgia is right, Quincy," said Mrs. Ramirez. "We don't want the worms inside the bin to crawl out during the parade."

Nancy could see George wrinkle her nose. Not because of the worms, but because she hated her real name—Georgia!

"They're hard-working worms!" Quincy said. "I mixed them in the soil myself. First they eat the stuff in the bin, then they recycle it by going to the bathroom—"

"Too much information!" Nadine Nardo cut in.

"Quincy, your compost bin in back of the school is a hit," Mrs. Ramirez said. "It just can't be on the float."

"Then I hate this parade," Quincy muttered to himself. But Nancy heard him loud and clear.

"Okay, everybody," Mrs. Ramirez said. "The time has come to announce the King or Queen of Green!"

Nancy grinned at Bess and George, who were grinning too. This was the moment they were waiting for!

Mrs. Ramirez held up a small piece of paper. "As I said, all of your essays were great. But the best one was written by . . ."

"Pick me . . . pick me . . . pick me," Nancy murmured. She squeezed her eyes shut and crossed her fingers. She tried crossing her toes, too, but her shoes were too tight!

"Felicity Faulkner!" Mrs. Ramirez announced.

Felicity jumped up from her seat. She pumped her fist in the air and shouted, "Yay, me!"

Nancy's heart sank. But no one was as upset as Deirdre.

"But Mrs. Ramirez!" she said. "Felicity just wrote an essay. I wrote a whole page about it on my own website, Dishing with Deirdre! I even had a message board where kids wrote how great my website was. And how I should be queen!"

"What for?" Tommy muttered. "You're already a princess."

"I heard that, Tommy Maron!" Deirdre snapped.

"Deirdre, sit down, please," said Mrs. Ramirez. "There are other things you can do besides being queen."

"Like what?" Deirdre asked.

"You can be in the recycled fashion show," Mrs. Ramirez suggested, "and make old clothes look new again!"

"Wear old clothes?" cried Deirdre. "The oldest clothes I have are six months old!"

"Give me a break!" George groaned under her breath.

Mrs. Ramirez went on about the float. There would be a recycled-items musical band. Kids would play instruments made out of empty bottles and cans. And everyone in the class would get to decorate the float for the parade.

"And my throne," Felicity said, waving her arm. "I want it to be fit for a queen!"

Nancy didn't feel bad anymore about not being queen. She couldn't wait to work on the float with her best friends.

"I can't wait to build our float," Bess said later during recess. "I can fix or build anything, you know."

"Maybe we can decorate the float with recycled computer parts!" said George, her dark eyes flashing. "What do you think of that?"

"As long as they're not from *my* computer." Nancy giggled. She knew George was a computer geek. Bess and George were cousins, but not at all alike. Bess had long blond hair and loved girly-girl clothes. George had curly dark hair. She loved clothes too—as long as they were comfy enough to do cartwheels in.

As the friends walked to the swings, they passed Deirdre, Nadine, and Madison Foley. The three girls had been chosen to be the recycled fashion models. But they were not talking about clothes. They were talking about Felicity.

"Some queen!" Madison was saying. "She doesn't even flush the toilet."

"Remind me never to go to her sleepover!" Deirdre scoffed.

George shook her head as the models strutted away. "Those things they said about Felicity were mean!" she said.

"I know!" said Nancy. But then she smiled. "Just for that, let's build Felicity the best throne ever!"

Bess nodded and said, "We can find some old

material and cover a chair with it. Maybe red velvet."

The girls ran to ask Mrs. Ramirez if they could see the float in the back of the school.

"Sure," Mrs. Ramirez told them. "But it's still just a flatbed truck."

"Not for long!" said Bess.

Nancy, Bess, and George ran around the school to the back. They could see Quincy stirring his compost bin with a long shovel.

Then they saw the float, already covered with bright green felt. In the middle of the truck stood a chair.

"That's going to be the throne," Nancy guessed.

"What's that on the chair?" asked George.

She hoisted herself up onto the flatbed truck. Then she picked a bottle up from the chair.

"It's probably a recycled bottle," Nancy guessed. "Somebody must have left it for our float."

"They also left a note," George said. She shook

the bottle upside down until a piece of paper dropped out.

"A note in a bottle?" Bess gasped. "Read what it says, George."

Nancy was curious too. She listened as George read the note out loud. "It says, 'Queen of Green . . . come clean!'"

Nancy wrinkled her nose.

What did *that* mean?

ChaPTER TWO

Mystery Note

"It's probably a note for Felicity," George said, jumping down from the float. "But what does it mean by 'come clean'?"

"Come clean means confess," said Nancy. "But what did Felicity do wrong?"

Nancy wanted to ask Quincy if he'd seen anybody put the bottle on the chair. But when she turned toward his compost bin, he was gone.

"Maybe we should show the note to Felicity," George suggested.

Nancy shook her head as she folded the note and slipped it into her jacket pocket. "It might spoil her fun about being queen," she said. "But we should keep it just in case."

"In case of a case?" Bess asked.

"Maybe," said Nancy. But she didn't think the note was a case for the Clue Crew—at least not yet!

As the girls turned to go back to recess, they saw a bunch of kindergartners. They were holding plastic pails and staring at the float.

Nancy recognized Quincy's little brother, Emmett. He was holding a pail too.

"What are you doing? And where's your teacher?" she asked him.

"She's over there. She said we could go and dump food mush in my brother Quincy's compobin if we stayed together," Emmett replied. "We can't wait to see all those neat worms!"

A girl in a pink jacket pointed to the float. "First let's climb up on that!" she said.

The kindergartners began charging toward the float, until George yelled, "Stop!"

"Why can't we climb it?" asked Emmett.

"Because it's our float," Nancy said. "We're going to decorate it for the parade."

"Big deal!" called a boy with freckles, flapping his hands. "We're *marching* in the parade!"

"Then why don't you march back to recess?" George asked.

"Okay!" Emmett said. He turned to his friends and shouted, "Company . . . forward—march!"

The kindergartners began stomping their feet. Chanting, "Hup, hup, hup," they marched their way around the school.

"They forgot to dump their compost," Bess pointed out.

"And we forgot about recess!" Nancy said.

But as they left the float, Nancy glanced over her shoulder. Who wrote the mysterious note to Felicity? And what did she have to come clean about?

"Daddy, don't throw away my broccoli scraps!" Nancy said that night after dinner.

"Why not?" Mr. Drew asked, holding a plate over the kitchen trash can. He and Nancy were clearing the table.

"I can throw them into Quincy's compost bin tomorrow," Nancy explained. "The worms will eat and recycle them!"

"Worms?" said Mr. Drew. He gave Nancy a little wink. "At least someone is eating their vegetables."

Hannah Gruen smiled as she loaded plates into the dishwasher. "I can put the broccoli in a plastic bag for you, Nancy," she said. "Just don't mistake the compost for your lunch."

"Eww, gross!" Nancy laughed.

Hannah, the Drews' housekeeper, had been making Nancy laugh since she was three years old and her mother had died. Hannah could never take the place of Nancy's mother, but she came pretty close!

"Guess what?" said Nancy. "Bess, George, and I found a mysterious note on the Queen of Green's throne today."

"Do you know who wrote it?" Mr. Drew asked.

"The only person I can think of is Deirdre,"

Nancy replied. "She was mad that she wasn't picked to be queen."

"Maybe Deirdre just needed to blow off some steam," Hannah suggested.

Nancy nodded. She had decided not to tell Felicity about the mysterious note. Besides . . .

"Whoever wrote the note was being earth-friendly, too!" Nancy said.

"In what way?" asked Mr. Drew.

"They reused the bottle for the note," Nancy said with a smile. "And both the bottle and the paper can be recycled."

"Our float is going to be the best part of the parade!" Nancy told Bess and George.

It was the first day of Earth Week. The kids were sliding their trays along the metal ledge in the lunchroom. They had been working on the float for a few days now and it was looking good.

Nancy, Bess, and George had finished decorating Felicity's throne that morning. Bess had brought in her grandmother's old red velvet coat to cover the chair. Hannah had given the girls a string of gleaming white pearls she no longer wore. They weren't real pearls, but they looked awesome draped over the back of the throne.

"It looks so regal!" Felicity had swooned.

"Wait till you see your crown," Tommy said. "I'm making it out of recycled dog food cans."

"Dog food?" Felicity gulped.

"Don't worry," said Tommy. "My dog licked them all clean!"

Deirdre, Madison, and Nadine spent the morning painting hats made out of jumbo tin cans with smooth safety edges. By the time they went to lunch, their hands were streaked with paint.

"Hey, supermodels," Mrs. McGillicuddy, the head lunch lady, called. "You'd better wash your hands or you'll be painting your veggie burgers!"

"Okay," Deirdre said with a little giggle.

Nancy watched as Deirdre and her friends left the lunchroom. "Deirdre doesn't seem mad anymore about not being queen," she said.

"Deirdre may be over it," said George. "But the Queen of Green is acting like a royal pain."

"A royal pain?" Nancy repeated. She looked to see where George was pointing. Felicity was standing by the trash cans.

"Oh, no you don't!" Felicity snapped at a second grader. "That water bottle needs to be recycled!"

"Who made you boss?" the boy asked.

"That's 'queen' to you, bucko!" Felicity snapped.

Felicity marched to the lunch counter, where Mrs. McGillicuddy was handing a veggie burger plate to Nancy.

"Is that one of those foam plates?" asked Felicity. "And are those plastic water bottles you're giving out?"

"Yeah, so?" Mrs. McGillicuddy said.

"Foam plates can't be recycled," Felicity said. "And plastic bottles take a thousand years to break down!"

Then she pointed at Mrs. McGillicuddy and announced, "The Queen of Green declares you guilty of trash treason!"

"Okay, Your Majesty," Mrs. McGillicuddy said coolly. "Now give me your tray so I can give you a veggie burger."

"No, thank you," Felicity said. "I always bring my own organic sandwiches to school in a one hundred percent recyclable brown paper bag."

"Hey, Felicity!" Trina shouted from the back

of the lunch line. "Be like an organic tree and leave. We're hungry!"

"Hmph!" said Felicity as she huffed away.

"I see what you mean," Nancy whispered to George.

Mrs. McGillicuddy scooped sweet potato fries onto the girls' trays.

"Who was that kid anyway, Iris?" another lunch lady asked Mrs. McGillicuddy.

"I don't know, Sylvie," Mrs. McGillicuddy said. "But she'll never say that again. She's in for a big surprise!"

Nancy, Bess, and George traded looks. What surprise?

The girls forgot about Mrs. McGillicuddy as they ate yummy veggie burgers and sweet potato fries. When lunch was over, it was time to get back to work.

Nancy and her classmates talked excitedly as they followed Mrs. Ramirez out of the building. But when they neared the float behind the school, they froze one by one.

Nancy stopped too when she saw their float. Felicity's throne was not just covered with pretty red velvet—it was covered with garbage!

"My throne!" Felicity cried. "Someone dumped trash all over my throne!"

Chapter Three

Trash Trouble!

Nancy's mouth hung wide open as she stared at the trashed throne. It was dripping with goopy brown and green stuff. The beautiful red velvet had clumps of white gook stuck to it.

"Who did this?" Felicity wailed.

But Felicity wasn't the only one who was upset.

"What if it happens *again*?" asked Kayla Bruce.

"Yeah," Kendra Jackson said. "What if our whole float is ruined right before the parade?"

Everyone began talking at once.

"Let's take a recess, class," Mrs. Ramirez said. "I'm going to find the custodian and ask him to help clean the throne."

On most days Nancy, Bess, and George would love an extra recess. But this time they were too stunned to have fun.

"I think the creep who trashed Felicity's throne also wrote that mysterious note," George said as they walked through the school yard.

"It's my fault!" Nancy groaned. "I should have showed that note to Felicity or to Mrs. Ramirez."

Bess saw Felicity running over. "Here she comes. Maybe you can tell her now."

But Nancy shook her head. "No!" she whispered. "If Felicity finds out I didn't show her the note, she'll hate me!"

"Okay, okay. My lips are zipped!" Bess promised.

Felicity was frowning as she hurried over. "You're detectives, right?" she said. "You've got to find out who trashed my throne."

"But we don't have a clue!" Nancy said.

"Yeah," Bess chimed in with a shrug. "The only clue we have is that weird note we found—"

Nancy clapped her hand over Bess's mouth.

But it was too late!

"Note? What note?" Felicity asked.

"Sorry, Nancy," said Bess. But with Nancy's hand over her mouth it sounded more like, "Pffrorrrphy, Nmmphy!"

Nancy dropped her hand. She then pulled the note out of her backpack and showed it to Felicity. "This was on your throne a few days ago," she explained.

Felicity's eyes popped open as she read the note. "Why didn't you tell me?" she asked.

"I thought it might make you feel bad, and you were so excited about being queen," Nancy admitted.

Nancy still felt awful. It was too late to stop someone from dumping on Felicity's throne—but it was not too late to help!

"Don't worry, Felicity," Nancy said, patting her shoulder. "We'll find out who did it."

"You will?" Felicity cried.

"We will?" Bess and George asked at the same time.

But Felicity was already jumping up and down.

"Thanks, you guys!" she said. "If you find out who did this, I'll do you a humongous favor too!"

"You will?" Bess asked.

"Like what?" George asked.

"You can be my ladies-in-waiting on the float!" Felicity said. "All queens have ladies-in-waiting!"

"Great," George muttered.

But Nancy got right down to business. She pointed to the note and asked, "Do you know what 'come clean' means, Felicity? Is there anything you did wrong?"

Felicity looked surprised. Then she quickly shook her head.

"No," she said. "All I know is that somebody hates me—and you have to find out who it is!"

So after school the Clue Crew did what they always did at the start of a new case—they headed straight to their detective headquarters in Nancy's bedroom.

George sat at the computer, opening a new case file, while Nancy examined the mysterious note. Bess stood by Nancy's closet, trying on her shoes.

"Okay," Nancy said, putting the note down. "What do we know so far?"

"That your new spring shoes are fabu-mazing!" Bess declared, wiggling her foot.

"She means what do we know about the case, Bess!" George groaned.

"We know the throne was trashed during lunch," Bess said. "We worked on the float that morning and everything was fine."

"Timeline: lunchtime," George said as she typed.

"But who would want to ruin Felicity's throne?" Nancy wondered out loud.

"Someone who hates Felicity," George guessed.

Nancy tapped her chin with her finger. It always helped her to think.

"Deirdre was mad at Felicity for winning the contest," she said. "Also, she and her friends left the lunchroom to wash their hands. They could have sneaked outside and dumped the garbage on the throne."

"Deirdre Shannon and the supermodels," George said out loud as she typed. "Our first suspects."

"Who else was mad at Felicity?" asked Nancy.

"I know!" Bess waved her hand. "Remember what Mrs. McGillicuddy said in the lunchroom?"

"Yes!" Nancy said. "She said that Felicity was in for a big surprise. Maybe the surprise was her ruined throne."

"But Mrs. McGillicuddy is the head lunch lady," George pointed out. "She would never leave the lunchroom during lunch."

"Unless some other lunch ladies did the job," Nancy said.

"And there's plenty of food in the kitchen to dump on the throne," Bess added. "A lot of it's yucky, too!"

"Write that down, George," Nancy said.

"Okay." George sighed. "But if we stop getting

extra desserts in the lunchroom, don't blame me."

Nancy smiled as she studied the case file. Two suspects already—not too shabby. Now all they needed were some more clues from the scene of the crime.

Nancy got permission from Hannah to walk her puppy, Chocolate Chip, to the school. She and her friends were allowed to walk up to five blocks from their houses as long as they walked together. And the school was exactly five blocks away.

When they reached the float behind the school, Nancy pointed to the throne. The dirty velvet cover had been taken off. All that was left was a naked chair.

"There goes our evidence," George said with a sigh.

But the Clue Crew didn't have to look far to find more clues. There on the green felt were smudges of red, yellow, and blue paint!

"How did those get there?" Bess asked.

"Deirdre, Madison, and Nadine were painting

their hats today," said Nancy. "Their hands were covered with paint when they left the lunchroom."

The leash tugged as Chip scurried under the float.

"Chip, come out now!" Nancy called.

Chip finally scampered out, a red sneaker dangling from her mouth.

"Do you think that's a clue?" Bess asked as Nancy pulled the sneaker from Chip's mouth.

"Maybe," said Nancy. "The models were wearing old clothes made to look new. This could have been part of an outfit."

"Deirdre wearing an old sneaker?" George laughed.

"As if!" Bess laughed too. Suddenly—

"Woof!"

Nancy turned to see Chip barking at a row of trash cans. But as she looked closer, she saw tall leafy stalks, bobbing up and down over the lids!

"What . . . is . . . that?" Nancy asked slowly.

"It looks like . . . giant broccoli or celery!" George said.

"Omigosh!" Bess shrieked. "They're giant walking veggies—and they're alive!"

CHAPTER FOUR

Art Smart

Chip barked louder as Bess kept screaming. The leafy green stalks ducked out of sight around the corner. Chip broke free from Nancy's grip. Still barking, she ran toward the trash cans. Nancy and George ran too. They looked behind the trash cans but saw nothing.

"Maybe we were just seeing things," Nancy said.

"Or they were seeing *us*!" George said.

It was getting late. The girls walked home and said good-bye to one another, promising to work on the case the next day.

Back at home, after helping Hannah sprinkle crunchy noodles on the tuna casserole, Nancy went upstairs to her room.

First she did her math homework. She was able to solve every math problem except one. But her biggest problem was figuring out who had messed up Felicity's throne.

Nancy hoped Deirdre, Madison, and Nadine hadn't done it. Deirdre could be a princess sometimes, but she wasn't mean—she did invite Nancy, Bess, and George to her sleepovers.

"Deirdre likes being a model," Nancy told Chip, who was sitting at her feet. "Maybe she's over the whole queen thing."

Chip nibbled lightly at Nancy's shoe while Nancy opened up Deirdre's website, Dishing with Deirdre. There on the main page were the words, "Ten reasons I should have been the Queen of Green!"

"Number one: Queen Deirdre sounds better than Queen Felicity," Nancy read out loud. "Number two: Felicity's favorite color is red. My favorite color is *royal* blue."

Nancy stopped there. She had read enough.

"Oh, well." She sighed. "I guess Deirdre *isn't* over it."

"I *thought* Deirdre did it!" George said the next morning. "I think we should tell Mrs. Ramirez right now."

The girls were hanging up their jackets before class. Nancy had just told Bess and George all about Deirdre's website and her ten reasons.

"We can't tell anyone yet," Nancy whispered. "We still haven't questioned Deirdre and the other models."

"What are we waiting for?" said Bess. She nodded at Deirdre, Madison, and Nadine hanging their jackets on nearby hooks.

Nancy didn't

like questioning friends. But as her dad once said, friends sometimes make mistakes too.

The girls walked over to the three models. Nancy smiled at them and said, "Can we ask you something?"

"Let me guess!" Madison giggled. "You want our autographs!"

"Why would we want your autographs?" asked Bess.

"Because we're famous supermodels, that's why!" Nadine said, striking a glam pose.

"We don't want your autographs," Nancy said. "We want to know if you know anything about the throne."

"You mean, did I dump trash on it?" Deirdre demanded.

"Well . . . yeah," Nancy admitted.

"We found spots of paint on the float," Bess said. "And you models were painting your hats, so—"

"We weren't the only ones who were painting yesterday!" Madison insisted. "Lots of kids had arts and crafts—and dirty hands, too."

Nancy thought Madison had a point. But it wasn't enough.

"Where are the hats you painted?" Nancy asked.

"If you must know, they're drying in the art room," Deirdre said, rolling her eyes. She turned to Madison and Nadine. "Come on, girls. Let's practice our turns!"

Nancy watched as the supermodels sashayed away. "Too bad we can't look at their hats in the art room."

"Who says we can't?" George said.

Nancy and Bess followed George to Mrs. Ramirez's desk.

"I'd like to go to the bathroom, please, Mrs.

Ramirez," George said. "I picked Nancy and Bess to be my buddies."

"Why two buddies?" Mrs. Ramirez asked.

"Um . . . because we're going to save water by washing our hands in the same sink!" replied George.

Mrs. Ramirez thought about it, and then she smiled and said, "That's a good idea. Go ahead, girls."

Nancy, Bess, and George left their classroom and hurried down the hall to the art room. Slowly Nancy opened the door. Mr. Kaplan, the art teacher, was not in the room.

"Come on," Nancy whispered.

The girls scurried into the room. They walked around the easels and craft tables until Nancy spotted three painted cans on the windowsill. They were decorated with feathers, sequins, and pieces of felt.

"Those are the hats!" said Nancy.

"Ooh!" Bess swooned. "Pretty!"

Before Nancy could stop her, Bess grabbed a hat and stuck it on her head. She giggled as she strutted around the room.

"And here eez Bess," George said with a French accent. "Looking bee-oo-tee-ful in a spaghetti-sauce can!"

"Take it off, Bess," Nancy urged. "Before Mr. Kaplan gets back."

Bess reached up. She put both hands on the tin can hat and began to pull.

"I can't!" she grunted.

"What do you mean you can't?" asked Nancy.

"I can't—because it's stuck!" Bess wailed.

ChaPTER FiVE

Royal Flush

"Oh, no! Let me try!" Nancy said. She ran to Bess, grabbed the tin can hat on her head, and began to pull. The can had smooth safety edges, but that didn't stop Bess from crying out.

"Owww!" she said. "You're pulling off my head!"

Nancy gave the tin can hat a big yank and it popped off. With the hat still in her hands, she stumbled back and slammed right into—

"Deirdre!" Nancy gasped. The models were in the room!

"Mrs. Ramirez said we could check on our hats," Deirdre said. "But what were you doing with mine?"

"We wanted to check out your hats too," Nancy explained.

"Because you still think we trashed the throne," said Deirdre. "Give me one good reason why we would want to ruin our own float."

"Because you were mad at Felicity for getting to be the Queen of Green," Bess said.

"That's a good reason," said Madison.

Deirdre glared at Madison. Suddenly Nancy noticed something about the tin can hat. It was painted pink, purple, and spring green. She looked at the other hats on the windowsill. They were the same colors!

"Bess, George," Nancy said. "Check out the colors of the hats. They're not the same as the smudges on the float."

"The smudges were red, blue, and yellow," Bess remembered.

"Told you!" Deirdre exclaimed. "Why would we want to touch all that garbage, anyway?"

"We don't even clean the class hamster cage when it's our turns!" Madison added.

"I mean—ick!" Nadine cried.

Nancy thought they had a point. She also thought Deirdre and the models were innocent.

"Here, Deirdre," she said. She handed her back the hat. "Sorry we accused you."

But when Deirdre looked down at her tin can hat, she cried, "Look what you did—you got your handprints on my hat. It was still wet!"

The door opened, and in walked Mr. Kaplan. He was wearing a blue smock, but he did not wear a smile when he saw all six girls in the art room.

"What are you girls doing in here without a teacher?" he asked.

Nancy was about to say something when Deirdre stepped forward.

"Mr. Kaplan, Mr. Kaplan!" she said. "Nancy just got handprints all over my hat!"

Nancy thought she'd be toast.

Until George came to the rescue. "What a cowinky-dink! Handprint designs are what all well-dressed women are wearing this year!"

"Seriously?" Deirdre asked.

"Sure!" said George. "Handprints are all over the Paris runways."

"Then I want handprints too!" Madison declared.

"So do I!" Nadine chimed in.

While Madison and Nadine pressed their handprints all over their hats, Nancy, Bess, and George left the art room.

They stopped at the bathroom so Nancy could wash the paint off her own hands.

As Nancy washed her hands, she heard a toilet flush . . . once, twice—three times!

"Someone is wasting water big-time," Nancy whispered to Bess and George.

The girls turned toward the bathroom stall where the endless flushing came from. The door opened, and out stepped Felicity!

Nancy's eyes popped wide open. The Queen of Green—wasting water?

"Hi, guys!" Felicity said. She walked over to a sink and turned on the water full blast. "Any news on the case?"

Felicity's bathroom buddy, Marcy, was at a sink too. "I heard you're going to find out who ruined Felicity's throne," said Marcy.

"We don't think it was Deirdre or the other models," Nancy reported. "The paint on their hats didn't match the paint we found on the float."

"They wouldn't touch garbage, either," Bess added.

"Well, keep trying, please," Felicity said. "Someone out there hates me!"

"I don't," said Marcy with a smile. "I like being friends with a queen."

Felicity dried her hands with an enormous wad of paper towels. She left the water running as she went out of the bathroom with Marcy. Nancy ran to the sink to shut it off.

"Did you see that?" Nancy cried.

"I saw it, but I don't believe it," said George. "First Felicity wastes water, then paper—then more water!"

"But Felicity and her family are supposed to

be so green," Bess said. "That's what she wrote in her essay."

"Unless," Nancy mused, "her essay was more fiction than fact."

"You mean she might have lied?" George asked.

"How can we find out for sure?" said Bess.

"There's only one way to find out," Nancy said, lowering her voice. "We have to go to Felicity's house after school. That way we'll see if they really are green."

The rest of the day went by quickly. After school the girls called their parents to ask for permission to take a walk. That walk allowed Nancy, Bess, and George to secretly follow Felicity home. They hid behind a tree trunk and watched Felicity skip into her house.

"Let's wait a few seconds before we ring her bell," Nancy whispered. "Or she'll know we followed her."

Just then Nancy saw Quincy. He and his little

brother, Emmett, were walking into the house
next door.

"I didn't know Felicity was Quincy's next-door
neighbor," said Nancy.

"There's a lot we don't know about Felicity,"
George said. She stepped out from behind the
tree. "Our few seconds are up. Let's do it."

Nancy, Bess, and George didn't want the Faulkners to know they were checking them out. So when Mrs. Faulkner opened the door, they pretended to be collecting recycled cans.

"Oh, we haven't recycled in ages," Mrs. Faulkner told them with a chuckle. "We just throw our cans and bottles in the regular trash."

Nancy looked sideways at her friends. The Faulkners didn't even recycle!

"Felicity is taking a shower now," Mrs. Faulkner said. "But you can wait for her in the family room."

Mrs. Faulkner pointed down the hall. As the girls walked toward the door at the end she called, "Turn on the TV or the CD player if you want. Or both!"

"Both?" Bess whispered when Mrs. Faulkner went back into the kitchen. "That's wasting tons of electricity!"

"So are all these lights that are on!" George observed, pointing around the room. "And it's still daytime."

"Felicity wrote in her essay that they use those curly fluorescent bulbs," Nancy said. "C . . ."

"CFL," George said. "Same initials as my aunt—Carol Felicia Landers!"

Nancy wanted to see if the bulb in one of the lamps was the CFL kind. She kicked off her shoes and stood on a chair underneath a lamp.

"Looks like the regular kind," she reported.

"What are you doing?" Felicity's voice asked.

Startled, Nancy fell off the chair. Luckily, the carpet was soft!

"Um . . . hi, Felicity," Nancy said, standing up. "We just wanted to see—"

"If we're really green?" Felicity cut in. Her hair was dripping wet from her shower.

"We saw you waste a lot of water and paper in school," Nancy admitted. "And with all these lights on, you're wasting tons of energy."

The Queen of Green turned bright red!

"Um—I just got soap in my eyes!" Felicity blurted. She began to blink. "So—I need a lot of light to see!"

"What about recycling your bottles and cans?" Bess asked. "Your mother said you never do it."

"Um, we never eat at home!" Felicity blurted again. "We always eat out. Pizza . . . with organic toppings!"

The girls each raised an eyebrow. Finally Felicity's shoulders drooped.

"Okay, I made up a few things in my essay," she confessed. "But I had to win that contest!"

"Why?" asked Bess.

"Because I'm the new kid," Felicity said. "Being Queen of Green would make everybody like me."

"Not if they found out you lied," Nancy

pointed out. "You are going to tell Mrs. Ramirez, aren't you?"

"Are you crackers?" Felicity exclaimed. "If I did that, she'd make somebody else queen!"

Nancy couldn't believe her ears. Lying on her essay was bad enough. But now Felicity wouldn't even correct her mistake!

"You guys aren't going to tell Mrs. Ramirez, are you?" asked Felicity.

"No," Nancy said. "That's your job."

Felicity heaved a big sigh.

"Oh, don't waste your time on me," she said. "Just find the person who ruined our float, once and for all!"

ChaPTER Six

Lunch Hunch

The next afternoon was a busy day. It was the day before the Earth Week parade, and everyone was busy practicing in the schoolyard. The fourth graders were blowing up blue and green balloons that looked like Planet Earth. The other third-grade class was practicing cartwheels for their Salute to Earth dance. But Mrs. Ramirez's class was busy putting the finishing touches on their Happy Earth Day to You! float.

"Good job, kids!" Mrs. Ramirez said as she stepped back to look at the float. "Everything seems to be in place!"

"Except my compost bin," Quincy said with a sigh.

Nancy, Bess, and George were filling empty bottles with pebbles to make instruments for the recycled band. From the corner of her eye, Nancy could see Felicity sitting on her throne.

"Do you think she'll confess?" Bess whispered.

Nancy watched Felicity smile and practice her royal wave. "I'll take a wild guess and say no," she whispered back.

"At least we know why somebody wrote that note to Felicity," said George. "But we still don't know who it was."

Nancy secretly pulled the mysterious note out of her pocket. As she unfolded it, she said, "Someone besides us knows that Felicity lied in her essay."

"Don't forget," Bess whispered, "we still have one more suspect. Mrs. McGillicuddy and the lunch ladies."

"Why would they write the note?" George asked.

"I don't know," said Nancy. "But the throne was covered with icky food stuff. And Mrs. McGillicuddy works in the lunchroom, so—"

"So maybe it was the same food that was served in the lunchroom that day!" George cut in.

"I remember we had veggie burgers and sweet potato fries," Bess said. "But I can't remember the food that was dumped on the throne."

"I know someone who will!" said George. "Scotty Patak!"

Nancy's eyes lit up. Scotty had the most awesome memory. He remembered everybody's birthday in the class. And the names of their pets!

The three girls walked over to Scotty, who was the conductor of the recycled-items band.

"Here are some more pebble-bottles," said George. The girls plunked the bottles on the float next to Scotty.

"Cool!" Scotty said. "How's your dog Chocolate Chip, Nancy?"

"Fine, thanks," Nancy said.

"Yo, Scotty!" called Peter. He was holding a drum made out of an old rubber tire. "How many times do I bang this?"

"It's bang the tire three times, shake the pebbles, toot the empty bottles five times, then the big finish!" Scotty called back.

Nancy was impressed. No wonder Scotty was picked to be the conductor!

"Scotty, remember the yucky stuff that was dumped on Felicity's throne?" Nancy asked.

"How could I forget?" Scotty said, wrinkling his nose.

"Do you remember what kind of food it was?" George asked.

"Let me think." Scotty squeezed his eyes shut. After a second he said, "Shredded lettuce, apple and pear cores, baked beans, carrot sticks, potato salad, and lots of peanut butter sandwich crusts!"

"Wow!" Nancy said. "Thanks, Scotty!"

"No problem." Scotty turned back to the band. "And a one—and a two—and—"

Nancy jumped as Peter pounded the rubber tire. Then she and her friends walked away from the recycled band.

"There was lots of peanut butter on the throne," Nancy whispered. "So let's find out if the lunchroom served peanut butter sandwiches that day."

Mrs. Ramirez gave the girls permission to go to the lunchroom. Bess said they needed more cans, which was true.

Nancy, Bess, and George ran through the back

entrance. Running in the halls was not allowed, so they walked quickly toward the lunchroom.

Once there the girls huddled against the wall and peeked inside. Nancy saw piles of cardboard boxes. "What are those for?" she whispered.

"Who knows?" George said, rubbing her nose. "All I know is that Mrs. McGillicuddy is serving fish sticks today. And fish sticks make me sneeze!"

The lunch ladies seemed to be in the back of the kitchen. Quietly Nancy waved her friends into the lunchroom. On the wall near the door was the weekly menu, tacked to a bulletin board. The girls studied it carefully.

"Hmm," Nancy said. "No peanut butter sandwiches the whole week."

"Or potato salad," George said.

"Or pears," added Bess.

Nancy heard Mrs. McGillicuddy's voice. She and her friends ducked behind the cardboard boxes and slowly peeked out. The lunch ladies were filing out of the kitchen.

Mrs. McGillicuddy was rubbing her hands

together as she said, "Good work, girls. Our top secret plan worked like a charm."

Nancy gave a little gasp. "Top secret plan?" she whispered.

Was Mrs. McGillicuddy talking about trashing Felicity's throne?

ChAPTER SEVEN

Write On!

"Why else would it be top secret?" George whispered. "Unless they did something . . . something . . . something . . ."

Nancy turned to stare at George. Her head was thrown all the way back. Her mouth was wide open as she said, "Ah, ah, ah—"

"Oh, no!" Bess whispered. "She's going to—"

"Ahh-chooooo!" George sneezed.

"Who's there?" called Mrs. McGillicuddy.

"Sorry," George sniffed.

The girls rose slowly from behind the boxes. Mrs. McGillicuddy folded her arms and said, "If you're looking for cookies, they're locked up in the kitchen."

"We're not looking for cookies!" Bess told her as they stepped out. "We're looking for peanut butter!"

Nancy and George stared at Bess. Was she about to tell Mrs. McGillicuddy they were looking for clues?

"Peanut butter makes a fabu-mazing organic glue!" Bess said with a smile. "And what's better for Earth Week than organic glue?"

But Mrs. McGillicuddy wasn't smiling. She was staring at the girls with wide eyes.

"There is no peanut butter on my watch!" she exclaimed. She walked over to the bulletin board and jabbed her finger on a memo. "Read that."

Nancy stood on her tiptoes and read the memo out loud: "Because of peanut allergies, peanut butter will no longer be served in the lunchroom."

Nancy checked the date on the memo. It had been written by the principal a whole year ago.

"Come to think of it," Bess murmured, "we haven't had peanut butter sandwiches for a long, long time."

"No peanuts on our yogurt parfaits, either," George added.

"You girls had better go back to your teacher," the pink-netted lunch lady said. "We've got a lot of work to do in here."

The girls turned to leave. But as they reached the door, George said, "One more thing, please."

"I told you—the cookies are locked up," Mrs. McGillicuddy grumbled.

"We don't want cookies," said George. "We just want to know what you meant by a top secret plan."

The lunch ladies stared at the girls. Then they began to laugh.

"If we told you, it wouldn't be a secret!" Mrs. McGillicuddy said.

As the lunch ladies kept laughing, Nancy whispered, "Let's go."

"I wanted to ask them what was in the boxes," Bess said once they were in the hall.

"Forget it, Bess!" said George. "Any more questions and we'll never get dessert again."

"And I don't think Mrs. McGillicuddy and the lunch ladies did it," Nancy concluded. "Whoever dumped trash on the throne had peanut butter. And they don't."

The three girls left the school. When they

returned to the float, Felicity was waiting for them.

"Well?" she asked. "The parade is tomorrow and you still haven't found out who ruined my throne."

"We're working on it," Nancy told her.

"Besides," George added, "you have a brand-new throne now. We worked hard on that, too."

"But what if it happens again before the parade?" Felicity wailed. "What kind of detectives are you, anyway?"

"The best!" Bess insisted.

"Then prove it!" Felicity hissed.

The girls watched the Queen of Green huff away.

"How can we prove it without suspects?" asked George.

"We can work on our clues," Nancy said. "Maybe we can recognize the handwriting on the mysterious note."

The girls studied the note. It was written in red ink. The penmanship was pretty neat.

"We can compare this to our essays hanging in the classroom," Bess suggested.

Nancy shook her head. "Half of them were written on computers," she said.

"Then we're out of luck." George sighed.

"That's what you think!" Bess said, her blue eyes flashing. "I'll be right back!"

Bess ran to the arts and crafts box. She came back with a big piece of orange construction paper in her hand.

"What's that for?" asked Nancy.

"We can't celebrate Earth's birthday without a birthday card," Bess explained.

"And birthday cards are signed!" George said. She nodded and smiled. "I get it, Bess."

"Hey, everybody!" Nancy shouted to her classmates. "Grab a pen and sign the birthday card!"

ChaPTER EighT

Name Game

Nancy smiled as the kids in her class signed the giant birthday card one by one. Soon they would have everyone's signatures!

"Do you think one of the signatures will match the handwriting on the note?" George whispered.

"We'll find out soon," Nancy whispered back.

Kayla Bruce was the last to sign the card.

"Thanks, guys!" said Nancy, picking up the card. "We're going to decorate it now."

But they were really going to investigate it.

"Good thinking, Bess," Nancy told her friend.

"Thank you!" said Bess with a smile. But then her smile turned into a frown, and she began to point. "L-look!"

Nancy turned to see where Bess was pointing. The same mysterious stalks and leaves were bobbing over some bushes.

"Omigosh!" Bess shrieked. "It's those walking veggies! And they're still alive!"

Bess grabbed Nancy's arm and made her drop the card on the ground. The stalks and leaves ducked out of sight. So did the card, as a strong wind blew it away!

"Get it!" shouted George.

Nancy, Bess, and George ran after the card as the wind swept it away. They chased the runaway card around the school into the school yard. When the wind died down, the card fluttered to a stop. But just as the girls were about to run to it—

"Hup . . . hup . . . hup!"

Nancy turned and gasped. It was the kindergartners. They were practicing their march— right in the direction of the card.

"Stop!" Nancy yelled.

The little kids kept marching. They were looking straight ahead.

"Hup . . . hup . . . hup!"

"Nooo!" Nancy cried as the kids marched over the card, ripping it to shreds. "Not the *caaaaaar-rrrrrd!!*"

The kindergartners marched away. Nancy, Bess, and George ran to pick up the pieces of the shredded card.

"It was my fault!" Nancy groaned. "I shouldn't have been such a klutz!"

"No, it was my fault," said Bess. "I shouldn't have grabbed your arm!"

"It was the wind's fault, okay?" George

snapped. "Let's save all these pieces before they blow away too."

The girls scooped up the torn pieces of construction paper and stashed them in their backpacks when they got back to their classroom.

After school the girls went straight to their detective headquarters. They sat cross-legged on the floor, putting the pieces of the ripped birthday card together.

"It's like putting Humpty Dumpty back together again," Bess said with a sigh.

The girls had managed to save all the pieces except one. But they had enough to study most of the signatures. Nancy compared them to the note one by one.

"Kendra Jackson . . . Kevin Garcia . . . Shelby Metcalf," George read the names. "Marcy Rubin . . ."

"Phooey," Nancy said, checking each one. "No match!"

"I bet the matching handwriting was on the missing piece," said Bess.

Nancy leaned back on her bed. "Now what do we do?" she asked.

"Check it out!" George exclaimed. She leaned over and peeled some paper from the bottom of Nancy's sneaker. It was orange. Written on it in red ink was Quincy's signature.

"The missing piece!" Bess said happily. "It was on the bottom of your sneaker the whole time, Nancy."

They compared Quincy's name to the

handwriting on the note. Nancy gave a big thumbs-up and said, "It's a match!"

"Why would Quincy write that note to Felicity?" George asked. "How could he know that she lied?"

"Easy," Nancy said. "Quincy is Felicity's next-door neighbor. If anyone would know about her family, he would."

"But even if he wrote the note," said Bess, twirling a lock of her blond hair as she thought, "where would he get all that gross stuff he dumped on her throne?"

The girls thought for a moment. Then at the same time they all said, "His compost pile!"

Nancy, Bess, and George walked the few blocks to Quincy's house. They found Quincy sitting on his doorstep, playing an electronic Game Buddy.

"Hi, Quincy!" Nancy called.

"Hey, what's up?" said Quincy, still staring down at his game.

"We didn't know you lived next door to Felicity," Nancy said. "Did you ever meet her family?"

Quincy looked up and stared at Nancy.

"Her family?" he blurted. "Why do you want to know?"

Nancy didn't like to trick suspects into confessing. But the parade was the next day, and time was running out.

"Felicity wrote how earth-friendly they all are," Nancy explained. "You're so lucky to have neighbors like them."

"Yeah, real lucky," Quincy sneered.

"I mean, they never waste water or electricity," George went on.

"And they must recycle everything!" Bess added.

"Yeah . . . everything," Quincy muttered.

"And I bet," Nancy said slowly, "they even have a bigger compost bin than yours."

Quincy jumped up.

"What?" he cried. He pointed with his game to the house next door. "Those Faulkners are the biggest polluters in River Heights. And Felicity is the biggest liar. Liar, liar, pants on fire!"

ChaPTER NiNE

Oh, Brother!

"So Felicity lied in her essay, huh?" George asked.

"Is that why you wrote this note you left for her?" Nancy asked. She reached out and showed him the note.

"How do you know it's mine?" Quincy asked.

"The writing on the note matched your writing on the giant birthday card," Nancy told him.

"Rats," Quincy said. "I should have known the Clue Crew was on the case."

"So you did write it?" asked Bess.

"Yeah," Quincy admitted. "One day I went to Felicity's house to watch TV with her. She played a CD at the same time. Then we drank juice out of plastic bottles, and when I went to throw mine away there was no recycling can!"

Quincy began waving his arms. "All the lights were on when it was still daytime," he went on. "And they did flush the toilet all the time. I heard it myself!"

"Is that why you wrote the note?" Nancy asked.

"I had to!" Quincy said. "When she wrote that bogus essay I had to let her know I knew the truth."

"But you didn't sign it!" said George.

"I didn't want to get in trouble," Quincy admitted. "I guess I was chicken."

"A nasty secret note is bad enough," Nancy said. "But did you have to dump stuff from your compost bin all over Felicity's throne?"

"Huh?" Quincy wrinkled his brow. "I didn't do that!"

"But you wanted your compost bin to be on the float, didn't you?" said Nancy.

"Not like that," Quincy said. "Besides, did you find any worms?"

"Worms?" Nancy asked.

"No—thank goodness!" Bess said.

"Then it couldn't have been my compost bin," Quincy exclaimed. "It's got a ton of worms."

Nancy looked at Bess and George. Quincy had a point.

Suddenly the door behind Quincy flew wide open. A flash of orange appeared in the door frame. It was Quincy's little brother Emmett, dressed in a carrot suit.

Emmett's arms were sticking out the sides, and on top of his orange hood was a tall stalk of green leaves.

"Hey, Quincy!" Emmett said. He held up a piece of paper. "Where are the magnets so I can hang this up on the refrig—"

Emmett stopped mid-sentence when he saw

Nancy, Bess, and George. His eyes went wide open as he said, "Uh-oh!"

The paper fluttered from Emmett's hand as he slammed the door shut. It blew off the door-step onto the grass.

"That was Emmett in his carrot suit," Quincy said, rolling his eyes. "The kindergartners are marching in the Earth Week parade dressed as organic fruits and veggies."

All Nancy could think about were the green leaves bobbing on top of Emmett's head. They looked like the strange leaves they'd seen behind the school!

When Nancy looked at Bess and George, she knew they were thinking the same thing.

"Why did he look so scared to see us?" Nancy asked.

"Who knows?" Quincy sighed. "He's been acting weird ever since he lost his sneaker."

"Sneaker?" Nancy exclaimed.

Before Nancy could ask if it was red, a woman's voice called from inside the house,

"Quincy, it's time to do your homework!"

"I'd better go inside," said Quincy. "Good luck with finding out who trashed the throne."

Quincy darted into the house and shut the door.

"Did you just see what I saw?" Nancy asked her friends.

"For sure!" George said. "The leaves on Emmett's carrot suit looked just like the leaves on the—"

"Walking veggies!" Bess finished for her.

"Quincy said the kindergartners are dressing up as fruits and veggies in the parade," Nancy said. "Maybe those weird leaves were them spying on us!"

"Why would they want to spy on us?" George wondered.

"I don't know," said Nancy. "But I think that sneaker we found belongs to Emmett."

George picked up the paper that Emmett had dropped. She held it up and said, "Hey, look!

This looks like the finger paintings we used to make in kindergarten."

But Nancy noticed something else. . . .

"Bess, George!" she said excitedly. "The paint is the same colors as the smudges we found on the float. Red, yellow, and blue."

"Look!" said Bess. She pointed to the bottom of the painting. "Emmett's teacher wrote his name and the date."

"It's the same date Felicity's throne was trashed," Nancy noticed.

The girls high-fived. In just minutes they had gotten a bunch of great clues.

"Let's find the kindergartners in the school yard tomorrow," Nancy said with a grin. "And catch them yellow, blue, and red-handed!"

Nancy couldn't wait to question the kindergartners. So the next morning, while the other kids played in the school yard, the girls searched for Emmett.

"Why do you think the kindergartners ruined our float?" George asked as they walked.

"Remember how they wanted to climb our float and we wouldn't let them?" Nancy said. "Maybe they were mad enough to do something mean."

"They could have had peanut butter, too," George added. "Kindergartners bring in their own lunch."

As they walked around the monkey bars, Nancy spotted Emmett. He was sipping from a juice box as he kicked a ball back and forth with two other kindergartners, the boy with freckles and the girl in the pink jacket.

"Hey, Emmett!" Nancy shouted.

Emmett looked up. His mouth dropped open. Then he looked at his friends and said, "Brendan, Emily, run!"

Leaving the ball, the kindergartners began to run. Nancy, Bess, and George ran after them at full speed.

"They've got to be guilty!" said George as they ran. "Why else would they be running away from us?"

Backpacks flapped as the girls and kindergartners darted through the school yard. As they ran past Felicity, she shouted, "Does this have anything to do with the case?"

"Yes!" Bess shouted back.

"I'm there!" said Felicity as she joined the chase.

The kindergartners were fast, but the third-graders were gaining speed.

77

"Hey! No juice in the school yard—and be careful!" a fifth-grade monitor shouted.

The kindergartners kept running, but not fast enough!

"Gotcha!" Nancy said, grabbing Emmett's backpack. But then Emmett whirled around and—

"Aaaaahhhh!" Nancy screamed.

Squirting into her eye from Emmett's juice box was something wet, sticky, and cold.

It was an apple juice ambush!

CHAPTER TEN

Hip, Hip, Parade!

"Quit it!" Nancy cried.

Emmett flung the juice box away.

"You little pest!" said George.

"I didn't mean to make it squirt!" Emmett exclaimed. "It was an accident!"

"Just like when he spilled gunk on your float!" Emily blurted. Her hand flew up to her mouth. "Whoops."

Emmett groaned under his breath.

"So you *did* ruin our throne," Nancy said. "Is that why you were spying on us in your veggie suits?"

"No!" said Emmett. "I was looking for my sneaker. I lost it when we jumped off the float."

"We didn't want you to know what happened," Brendan added. He leaned forward and began to whisper. "So we went in disguise."

"I didn't mean to mess up the float," Emmett explained. "But I tripped on an empty bottle. Then all the gooky stuff spilled out of my pail."

"What were you doing with all that gooky stuff?" Bess asked.

"It was stuff from our lunch we didn't eat," Emily said. "We wanted to throw it in Quincy's mush pile."

Nancy smiled at Bess and George. So that's how the throne got messed up—it was the kindergartners all along!

"You ruined my float!" Felicity told the little kids. "You'd better go tell our teacher, Mrs. Ramirez, what you did."

"No way!" Emmett gasped.

"Your teacher will tell our teacher!" said Emily.

Nancy had to think fast. "You might get the River Heights Elementary School Honesty Award," she said.

"The what?" Emmett asked.

"The school gives out an honesty prize every year," Nancy said. "Maybe you'll win."

The kindergartners exchanged smiles. Then Emmett said, "Let's find Quincy's teacher!"

They had started to run when Nancy called, "Wait!"

"Now what?" Emmett groaned.

Nancy pulled the red sneaker from her backpack. She held it up and said, "You forgot this."

"My sneaker!" Emmett cheered. "Thanks!"

After taking his long-lost sneaker, Emmett and his friends left to find Mrs. Ramirez.

"Wow," said George. "They're really going to tell Mrs. Ramirez."

"They're being real grown-up," Felicity said. "For kindergartners."

Nancy frowned when she heard that. She turned to Felicity and said, "They're more grown-up than you. At least they're telling the truth."

Felicity didn't reply.

As the day went by, the kids in Mrs. Ramirez's

class heard the good news. The Clue Crew had solved the case of the trashed throne.

At lunchtime Nancy and her classmates waited outside the lunchroom for the doors to open. They talked about their float and the parade.

"Now our float is safe," Nadine said, "thanks to Nancy, Bess, and George!"

"Way to go, Clue Crew!" Tommy cheered.

Deirdre shook her head and said, "What was Felicity thinking when she lied on her essay?"

"What was *Emmett* thinking?" Quincy sighed. "You don't put peanut butter and macaroni salad in a compost bin. Just fruit and veggie scraps, cut grass, leaves—"

"Hey, guys!" a voice cut in.

Everyone turned. Felicity was running down the hallway with a big smile on her face.

"Guess what?" she said. "I finally told Mrs. Ramirez that I lied on my essay."

"No way!" said George.

"Yes way," Felicity said, nodding. "And it feels great."

"Woo-hoo!" Quincy cheered. "The Queen of Green came clean—once and for all."

"Oh, Mrs. Ramirez said I can't be the Queen of Green anymore because I lied," Felicity said.

Nancy felt bad for Felicity. But she knew telling the truth was the best way to go.

"But guess what else?" Felicity asked. "I'm going to talk my mom and dad into saving water and electricity—and into recycling all our paper, cans, and bottles, too."

"That's great, Felicity!" Nancy exclaimed.

"I know," said Felicity. "But now that I goofed, who will be the Queen of Green on our float?"

All eyes turned to Deirdre.

"Don't look at me," Deirdre said.

The lunchroom door flew open. Mrs. McGillicuddy stood in the doorway wearing a green hairnet and a big smile.

"Attention all students!" she announced. "Changes have been made in the lunchroom!"

"Changes?" Nancy asked. "What changes?"

"If you'll notice, there are no more foam

plates!" Mrs. McGillicuddy said. "Instead of plastic water bottles, we have a brand-new water cooler with reusable cups."

Excited whispers filled the hall.

"And whatever fruits and veggies you don't eat will go right into that young man's compost pile." Mrs. McGillicuddy nodded at Quincy.

"Sweet!" Quincy shouted.

"So in honor of Earth Week," Mrs. McGillicuddy boomed, "we declare the River Heights Elementary School lunchroom officially green!"

A big cheer erupted from the students.

Mrs. McGillicuddy and the other lunch ladies waved the kids into the lunchroom.

"So that was Mrs. McGillicuddy's top secret plan," George said.

"To make the whole lunchroom earth-friendly!" Bess added. "How cool is that?"

Nancy watched as Mrs. McGillicuddy took her place behind the counter. She had done an awesome thing turning a whole lunchroom green in just a week. So awesome, it gave her an idea.

"You guys," Nancy said excitedly. "I think I just found our new Queen of Green."

"Happy Earth Day to you!" Nancy, Bess, and George sang together. "Happy Earth Day to yooooooou!"

Everyone was singing on Mrs. Ramirez's Earth Week float. That's because it was finally the day of the big parade, and all of River Heights Elementary School marched down River Street.

One first-grade class walked their pets in a parade of the species. There were dogs, cats— even an iguana walking slowly on a leash. The fourth graders volleyed their Earth balls back and forth, while some fifth graders pushed a car they'd built that ran on people power, not gas.

Marching in front of Mrs. Ramirez's float were the kindergartners in their fruit and veggie costumes, chanting in unison, "Hup . . . hup . . . hup!"

Nancy smiled as she waved at Hannah and

her dad, who were standing in the crowd. They both clapped and cheered.

"Fabulous float, Nancy!" Mr. Drew shouted.

"Thanks!" Nancy yelled back over the music.

Proudly Nancy looked around the class float. It *was* pretty fabulous. The cans and bottles were tied to the float with colorful ribbons. The recycled can and bottle band played while the recycled fashion models

struck glam poses. Felicity was one of them now.
She strutted back and forth in an old-made-new
dress with dangling recycled bottle-cap earrings.

Sitting on the lid of his compost bin was

Quincy. The kids in the class had finally agreed that an earth-friendly compost bin was definitely float-friendly, too—even with the worms. Mrs. Ramirez said it was okay, as long as Quincy kept the lid on very tight!

Behind Quincy sat the Queen of Green herself—Mrs. McGillicuddy!

"Hellooooo, River Heights!" Mrs. McGillicuddy shouted from her throne, waving a soup-ladle scepter. Instead of a hairnet, she was wearing a shiny crown made out of recycled silver foil. "Who says lunch ladies don't rule?"

But no one could be prouder than Nancy, Bess, and George as they stood side by side on the float.

"We solved another case, you guys!" said George over the music and cheers.

"And we saved our class float," Bess added.

Nancy beamed as she pointed to all the cans and bottles they'd collected. "Not only did we save our float, we helped save the earth," she said. "And that is the *best* part of all!"

Recycled Bottle Band Blast!

Soda Pop Quiz What's a fun way to recycle and reuse empty bottles?

Answer Turn them into earth-friendly musical instruments!

You Will Need:

Six empty bottles (plastic or glass)

Tap water

Five friends to join the band

❊ Fill the first bottle almost to the top with water. Keep filling the following bottles with less and less water until the last has about an inch or so of water in it.

Good Vibrations

❀ Blow over the tops of the bottles. Notice how each bottle has a different tone? That's because your breath is making the air inside the bottle vibrate. The less water, the deeper the pitch.

Band Together

❀ Get five friends to each play a bottle, and take one for yourself. Don't be afraid to experiment. Pour water in and out until you get the tune you're aiming for!

More Bottle Brainstorms

❀ Fill empty glass bottles with water. Instead of blowing across the tops, tap the sides of the bottles with a spoon. The less water, the higher the pitch.

❀ Or fill empty bottles with dried beans, birdseed . . . or rock on with pebbles! Cover the tops with masking tape, then shake it up for a neat maraca-like sound.

Help Nancy Solve the Case on Your Nintendo DS!

Family heirlooms are disappearing all over Twin Elms. The residents are counting on Nancy Drew® to solve the mystery before it's too late!

- Interview people and gather clues using the stylus to uncover the location of the hidden staircase.

- Explore the large and mysterious Twin Elms house and examine anything that is out of place.

NANCY DREW
THE HIDDEN STAIRCASE

Earn the top rank of Master Detective and find the stolen items!

Available Now!

Visit www.thq.com to learn more!